This Little Tiger book belongs to:

_____

_____

_____

For everyone at Little Tiger,
friends and family . . .
A very BIG thank you - J L

LITTLE TIGER PRESS
1 The Coda Centre,
189 Munster Road, London SW6 6AW
www.littletiger.co.uk

First published in Great Britain 2016
This edition published in Great Britain 2017

A CIP catalogue record for this book is available
from the British Library

Printed in China · LTP/1400/1739/1116

2 4 6 8 10 9 7 5 3 1

Jonny Lambert

THE GREAT
AAA-
Ooo!

LITTLE TIGER PRESS
London

As Mouse scampered homeward through the dark, rackety wood, a horrible howl was heard.

AAA-OOO!

AAA-OOO!

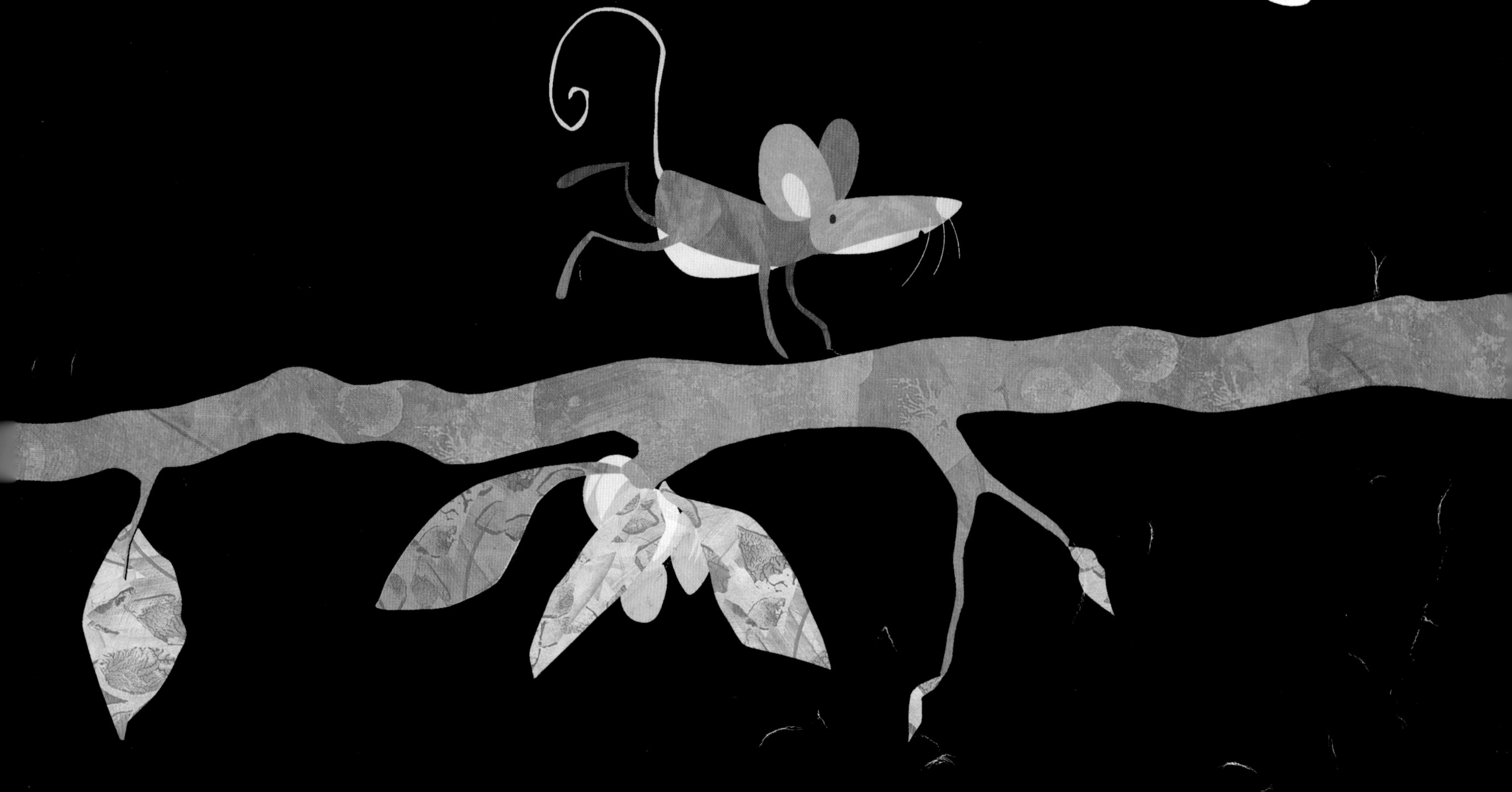

Owl winked one beady eye.
"Tu-whit tu-whoo, was that you?"

"Not I," squeaked Mouse nervously.
"I...I...I thought it was you!"

"Twaddle, not I!" hooted Owl.
"If it was not you, then who,
tu-whit tu-whoo, is making this
awful AA$_A$-O$_0$o?"

Bear grumbled up the tree, disturbed from
his slumber by the hullabaloo.
"Grrumph!" he grizzled. "Which one of you
made that awful AA$_A$-O$_0$0?"

"Not I!" Owl huffed. "I hoot and toot
and tu-whit tu-whoo."

"Nor I!" squeaked Mouse. "I scritch and scratch,
squeak and chew, but never ever
do I AA$_A$-O$_0$0!"

AA

KNOCK, SMACK, THWACK, Moose tapped on the tree. "Hey, you up there . . . yes you . . . you three! Are you making that horrible howl?"

"Not us," grunted Bear. "We growl, squeak and
tu-whit tu-whoo, but never ever do we **AAₐ-Oₒo!**"

"Then WHO?" bellowed Moose. "WHO!"
Closer and louder came the awful . . .

AAₐ-Oₒo!

AAₐ-Oₒo!

AAₐ-Oₒo!

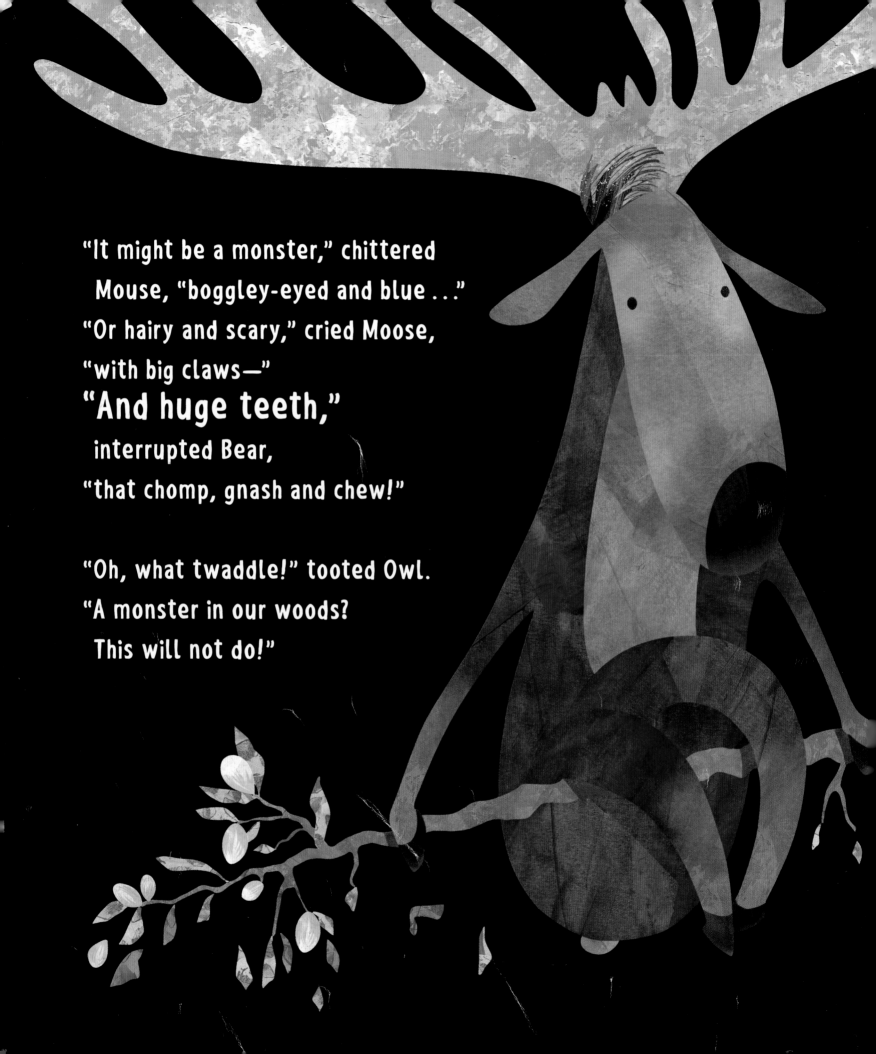

"It might be a monster," chittered
  Mouse, "boggley-eyed and blue..."
"Or hairy and scary," cried Moose,
"with big claws—"
"And huge teeth,"
  interrupted Bear,
"that chomp, gnash and chew!"

"Oh, what twaddle!" tooted Owl.
"A monster in our woods?
  This will not do!"

AAA-
OOo!

"It's a monster alright! What will we do?"
cried Moose, as Duck, Goose and Dove landed
with a startled QUACK, HONK and COO!

"Quick! Get up here!" growled Bear,
scooping Wolf Cub from the ground.
"Something scary is coming and it's
making a horrible sound!"

"Do monsters eat cubs?"
whimpered Wolf.

"Monsters eat everything!"
said Duck with a cry.

"We'll be plucked, stuffed,
and roasted, and put in a pie!"

"A pie?" roared Bear.

"Save yourselves!
Follow me!"

And the animals scrambled and
clambered higher up the tree.

The animals came crashing to the floor with a

HONK!

BELLOW!

HOOT!

COO!

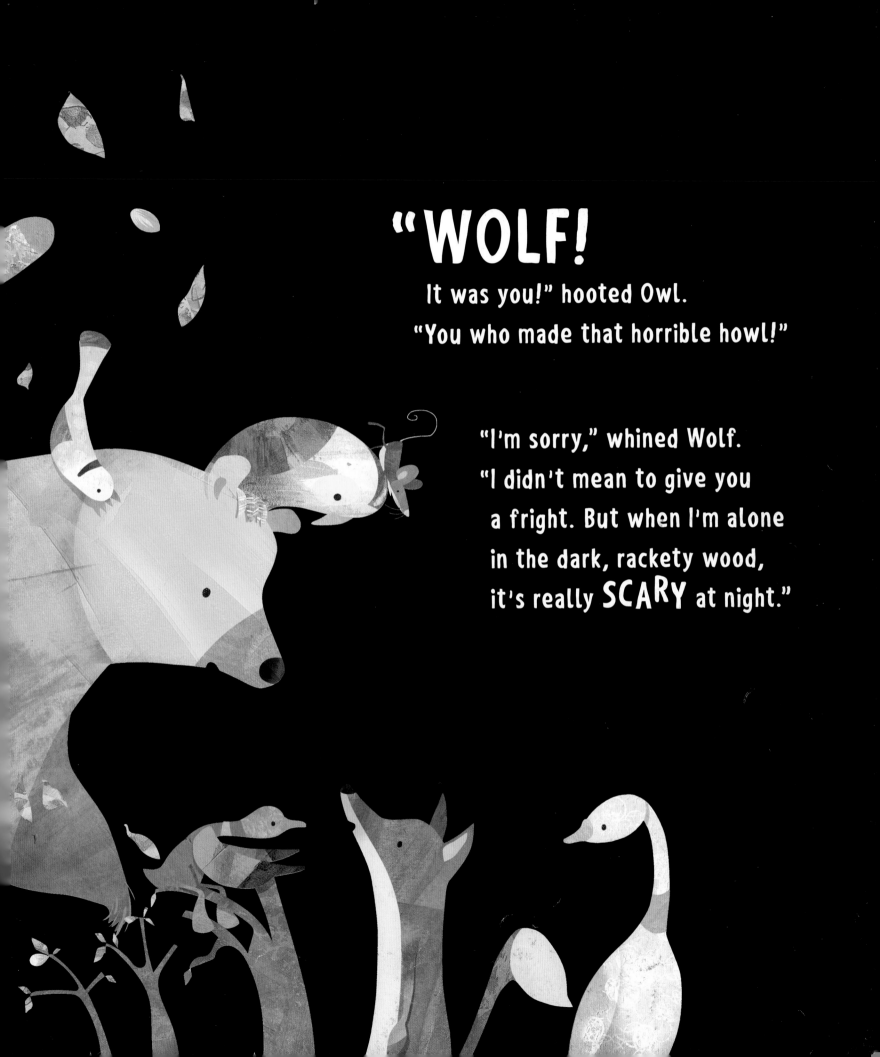

"WOLF!
It was you!" hooted Owl.
"You who made that horrible howl!"

"I'm sorry," whined Wolf.
"I didn't mean to give you
a fright. But when I'm alone
in the dark, rackety wood,
it's really SCARY at night."

Bear gave Wolf Cub a **mighty** hug.

"There, there ... it's alright.
If you promise to be quiet,
you can sleep with us tonight."

At long last, the rackety wood was peaceful once
more. The animals drifted off to sleep with a ...

SNUFFLE, WHEEZE, SNORE ...

SPLUTTER, MUTTER, GRUMBLE, COO,

MUMBLE, MURMUR ...

cock-a-d

oodle-doo!

I love you
more
and more

Nicky Benson
Jonny Lambert

Ooo!

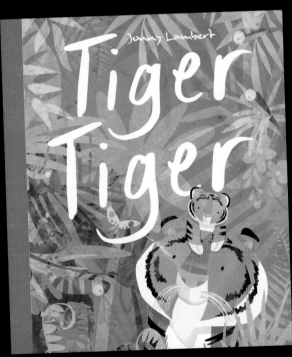

Jonny Lambert

Tiger
Tiger

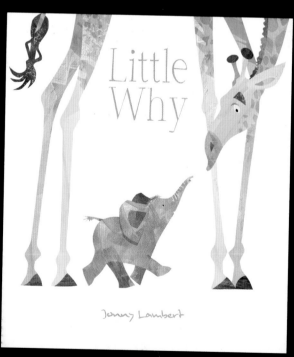

Little
Why

Jonny Lambert

More beautiful picture books by Jonny Lambert

For information regarding any of the above titles or for our catalogue, please contact us:
Little Tiger Press, 1 The Coda Centre, 189 Munster Road, London SW6 6AW
Tel: 020 7385 6333 · E-mail: contact@littletiger.co.uk · www.littletiger.co.uk